I0608277

Truth & Dare

Kornelia Blackmore

Published by Kornelia Blackmore, 2022.

This is a work of fiction. Similarities to real people, places, or events are entirely coincidental.

TRUTH & DARE

First edition. February 17, 2022.

ISBN: 978-1735307213

Written by Kornelia Blackmore.

I know no one ever reads these, and that's okay, but I wanna tell you this book was the HARDEST for me to write because I write way too many words.

But it's with that in mind I considered writing a short story to see if I could get it published. I did it, and I'm so proud of it.

So to everyone who ever encouraged me, and all the people who listened to me ramble, I appreciate you so much. You have no idea.

I hope you enjoy this short story I wrote, it was a fun treat. Many blessings and love friends.

Chapter 1: Reunited in Mess

Yumi

"Okay mom! I'm leaving!" I shouted while slinging my backpack over my shoulder and grabbed my suitcase handle, "Wait!" My mom shouted.

I turned and gazed at her over my shoulder since my friends were waiting for me to take this camping trip in the woods.

"Yeah?" I asked.

"Are you wearing your underwear?" She asked seriously.

I laughed, she always asked me that stupid ass question every morning to make sure I smiled. It worked cuz I love the corny shit my mom does. It's why she's my best friend in the entire world.

"Yes mom," I said grinning. Then I grabbed the handle of my suitcase & adjusted my backpack with stuff in it for the trip.

"Text me when you make it there safely!" She shouted.

"Will do!" I replied, shutting the door behind me.

The sun beamed in my eyes and was happily met with two glaring eyes standing in front of the grey SUV.

"Always the pretty girls that take the longest," my buddy Ares said rolling his eyes, "Fuck off, you're just jealous cuz I do care about my looks and grades," I joked walking towards him as he opened the trunk of the car to put my bags in it.

"Ugh! Can we just go already?? We're gonna hit traffic!" Phoebe said folding her arms across her tiny chest. She normally doesn't show her legs but it's why her light wash shorts look good on her olive skin. I couldn't help but smile at that little detail.

"Besides we still have to pickup dickhead," I reminded.

So my group of friends; Phoebe, Ares and my ex, Caleb. I have no idea why they still wanna bring him on this trip, he's only gonna make it hell for me, and have others remind me why we should be together.

It's done, it's over with. Not important anymore. Sure I still love him, but it's not enough. Not like it was back then, since we're not in high school anymore.

Something tells me they're gonna try and set us up, but whatever. I really could care less.

"Which is why we need to get moving!" Phoebe reminded hopping in the drivers seat.

Ares shut the trunk door to the car and I wrapped my arms around him in a warm hug. He smelled like cheap cologne but it smells good to me, I thought as he held me back.

I seriously love how he just does what he wants. Cuz he's bisexual and literally does not care.

In fact I've seen him tell a man straight to his face, I can suck your dick better than she can, and wink. With confidence. Not to mention he can fight. So yeah no, I learned a long time ago not to mess with my bestie.

It's been months since I've seen him, and it's why I couldn't hold myself back when I saw him.

"Hey you, how's my bitch doin? I missed yo pretty ass," he said nuzzling his face in the crevice of my neck and grabbed my ass cheek in one palm.

When did his hands get to be so big? I thought while laughing.

"Busy with school and missing your ugly ass face," I chuckled while tugging on his dark locs to mess with him. He hates it when I call them dreadlocks, so I learned not to anymore, I thought as he broke from me and tied his locs in a messy bun.

When did his hair get to be so long?

It's hard for me not to remember him as the scrawny, dorky black kid that got his ass beat a lot in high school.

Until one day, he just snapped & beat the bloody hell out of his bullies, and then emerged my arrogant, muscly, asshole whose been my bestie since then.

He walked towards the back seat, and I strolled to the front seat, hopped inside, & was happily greeted with Starbucks hot coffee in the holster.

Thank you Phoebe, you know me so well.

"Well that's cool and all, but going out with me would be so much better," he joked.

I swatted to hit him in the face, "fuck off Ares," I laughed.

"I would really enjoy that," he teased.

"Nope you got shit on your dick, no thanks," I laughed sipping my coffee.

Phoebe started the car, "Ugh guys! I hate sex talk! Can we please change the subject?" She whined and drove out of my driveway.

"Fine I'll leave it alone for now," Ares said leaning in the backseat.

"SEATBELT ON NOW!" Phoebe shouted.

He just laughed and did what she said.

"Okay Pheebs damn, it's just a seatbelt," he teased. Pheebs has always been the anxious neurotic one in our group, and while sure it's not a personality type but for her it is.

One day she'll break out of her shell, even though we've all been trying for years, since her parents are stupid strict.

But I guess since she's been getting good grades in her college classes, she was allowed to host this trip & we all split funds to pay for it. But Ares covered most of it.

I texted my mom to let her know we rolling out and that we still have to pickup my ex.

"Oh honey I know that sucks " she texted back.

"I know, tell me about it," I replied.

My moms the best.

"So what are you gonna do when you see him? I know that shit is gonna be so awkward for you," she replied.

"Honestly, I have no idea, more than likely I'll just keep it classy since I'm gonna be stuck in a car with him for God knows how long," I texted.

"You're better than me, I would've been kicked his ass especially for what he did, humiliating you like that in front of his rich ass family. Ugh I swear," she cursed.

I picked up my coffee & sipped more of it.

"You're not texting your mom again are you? When are you gonna grow up!" Ares plucked my ear & I smacked his hand away, "when you stop sucking dick how about that?" I giggled.

My mom always loved Ares and hated Caleb. Since Ares always fought other dudes that tried to approach me incorrectly. So he's saved my ass more times than I care to remember.

"Maybe when hell freezes over," he laughed, "exactly, so quit teasing me about my mom," I sneered.

"How is she?" He asked, "she too misses your ugly face & wants you to come see her soon. I swear if she didn't already mention a hundred times you're the son she never got to have," I replied.

"Daww she misses me! I miss her beautiful face too, seriously your mom is hot," he said.

I shot him a hard glare, "please don't do this to me, that's the last image I need of you right now."

"I'm just sayin," he admitted without a care like he usually does.

"I could NEVER talk to my mom about that kinda stuff like you do with your mom," Phoebe commented while sipping her iced coffee, making another turn down the street.

"Oh I know, you're mom is way too uptight," I replied.

"No she isn't, she just values being mindful of others!" Phoebe defended.

"But it's why your mom never liked me," Ares reminded.

"Because you asked how long it's been since she got laid!! That's REALLY disrespectful to elders!" Phoebe griped.

"I'm Jussayin, maybe she wouldn't be so uptight if she did get laid," he shrugged his shoulders.

"Now I'm inclined to kick your ass FOR Phoebe," I argued.

"Y'all not gonna win," he snickered.

His arrogance always pissed me off and it's why we would never work in a relationship. Even though people have always asked if we were together, despite how many years I've known this asshole for.

The only way I would consider it is if he grew up and learned how to be serious.

I've only seen him serious a few times and if I'm being honest, that's when he's actually really attractive to me, but I'll never admit that out loud.

Besides our friendship is more important to me. So I'll never actually say how attractive I always saw him even back in high school. It's why when we became friends I dropped that original idea all together.

But Caleb when I met him back then was nice and sweet. He never cared about his money or inheritance. Until one day he did & it's why he's stuck engaged to some bitch as a business deal.

I mean who gets married for business anymore? What is this the Stone Age?

Caleb never did tell me what changed his mind so quickly, anyways. But I don't care anymore.

He hurt me the worst way possible, and it happened at a big ass banquet where he introduced another girl as his fiancée and me as the fling when people asked why this "rat" was tagging along with him.

He didn't defend me at all, just looked away.

The whispers were too painful, so I walked as far as I could until I ended up calling Ares to come get me.

As soon as I saw him, I bawled, and told him that we broke up, but I never told him the reason why. Even when he nagged me about it, I still refused to tell him. And never will.

"You think I give a damn about winning a fight against you! It's the principle you ass hat," I cursed.

Phoebe laughed, "thanks girl, you've always had my back when it came to Ares being a jerk!" She giggled.

"Anytime love," I smiled.

"Please make out," he commented sticking his head in between the head rests.

"GOODNIGHT ARES!" Me and Phoebe said at the same time, laughing.

We blasted some tunes & started jamming to our oldies.

Music was always a thing for us; Ares loves soft rock & rap, I love pop & classic rock, and Phoebe loves compositional music, anime songs, J & K-pop.

Caleb always loved indie and underground music. So we always were a well rounded group.

We were only a few turns away before my stomach started churning with anticipation.

But I played it cool and went back to texting my mom.

"I know mom, it's cool. I was too upset to do any of that to be completely honest. But, it's not a big deal, I'll just keep it cool & ask how he's doing," I told her.

"Baby I know what that means, you are upset about it. If you are that's okay, you're allowed to feel what you feel, but you're right being cordial is more important at the moment. Just when you do get some alone time please punch him in the face for me, I love you. I'm here if you need me," she ended the conversation.

I smiled at her words, she doesn't know it but it's why I've never deleted my texting conversation with her so I could go back to the words she's given me over the years when I do feel like shit.

She's the one that greeted me at two in the morning, knowing she had work the next day with a tub of ice cream and a joint the night Caleb dumped me. It's why I spilled everything to her, and all she did was hug, and cry with me.

Cuz I know it's her way of sharing her emotions with me and it's why she's my best friend in the whole world.

"Thanks mom, love you too " I replied, locked my phone & then checked my makeup in the mirror to make sure I looked good.

If it's one thing my mom did teach me, it's to make a dude want you by looking good, knowing he can't have you cuz he fucked up.

Revenge is best served cold.

"Yo!" Caleb shouted opening the trunk door and tossed his bag in, "thanks for comin to get me, I honestly did not feel like being bothered," he laughed while hopping in the backseat with Ares.

I didn't look behind me, he's not worth it.

I did hear Ares dab him, "sup bro, how you been? Ain't heard shit from you in a minute," he said. But something was off about the way he said it, and I'm really not sure why.

"Been busy with bullshit, getting ready for graduate school, more class work & some other dumb shit," Caleb replied casually.

Or getting ready to be married, but I bet you ain't tell them that shit, I thought to myself while scrolling through my socials.

"Shit man that sounds about right, I've just been livin it up while busting my ass to get my BA. Work hard, party harder is my motto," Ares replied to Caleb.

"Yumi, Phoebe, how you guys been?"

Caleb asked in his usual "nice guy" tone.

"Hey Caleb, I've been good, just been trying to pass these damn classes," I said.

Still not looking back at him. I refuse to see that dimpled smile that always made my heart jump.

"You still taking Genetics?" He asked.

"Fuck that class," I argued.

"Well if anyone would like to know, I recently got an A on my English test!" Pheebs proudly announced moving so we could hit the highway.

"Well duh! Of course you would!" Ares joked.

"Hey what does that mean??" Phoebe asked.

"Hey Pheebs that's whassup! Congrats girl, I barely passed my last test in Genetics with a B plus," I spoke to stop her from arguing with Ares.

Their banter is always cute to me though.

It always made me wonder how come they never tried to date? But I guess that's cuz he's too much of a party animal for her, but that's why they say opposites attract.

I fluffed my straight black hair, "ugh, my hair literally has no volume at all," I complained.

"It's cuz you prolly ain't usin the right shit in it, fun fact, did you know that a dudes jizz can prevent wrinkles and smooth skin, so it makes for an amazing beauty product," Ares commented.

"Shut up Ares." I cursed, "I'm not even gonna start with how wrong that is,"

"The offer is always on the table," he reminded.

"Jeez just fuck already," Caleb joked.

But I knew he wasn't joking, it always bothered him whenever me and Ares hung out, and I don't get why, it's not like he didn't know him & wasn't friends with him either.

"Dick head," Ares replied.

Caleb shoved Ares like old times and it made my heart sink. I thought he would have changed somehow and it would be awkward and it wasn't. Which only made this whole situation even more gut wrenching for me.

Ugh, why me?

Chapter 2: My Little Shit

Yumi

Needless to say we made it to the cabins safely without either of us killing each other or without anyone asking us what happened. Which was considerate of them.

Between me and Caleb, we kept it casual with questions like; hows classes? Is your mom still a bitch? Etc. The only part that helps this entire situation was us being friends before we dated.

When we arrived, I hopped out of the car and was greeted with the scent of dewy grass and salt water from the river nearby. As the sun shone through the rustling leaves, I noticed the massive, wood style cabins, that all lined around each other in a circle, and a fire pit in the center.

Damn this was nice, and totally worth the money spent.

We were each supposed to get a cabin to ourselves, but there were only three instead of four. I paled, because that means there's only one bed in each of them since it was like a suite style.

I groaned to myself. I knew she would've set me and Caleb up like this, I just knew it.

"Pheebs," I said turning to face her, but she kept walking while dragging her pink bag behind her towards the cabin tucked away behind the trees, like she didn't hear me.

"Have fun!" She waved.

That wave told me everything I needed to know, but I claim dibs on the cabin closest to the river.

"Well I guess that means—" Caleb started to say looking in my direction, but Ares stepped in and wrapped his arm around my waist, "I'll share a bed with you," he joked.

"Not on your life," I rejected taking my bags towards the house on the opposite end.

"Aww come on! I got the drinks and smoke, pleaaase," he begged.

"I really don't mind staying with you Yumi," Caleb suggested.

"On second thought Ares can stay with me," I confirmed.

It's not that I didn't want to stay with Ares, it's just we're older now and not like in high school when he stayed in the guest room. And even that experience told me he's annoying to live with, even if it was a short time since he got into some shit back then.

"FUCK YES!" He shouted grabbing his bags and walked in front of me to the house. Since I held the door open, he walked inside and started placing his bags next to mine in the living room.

"Come inside wifey! I'll make the fire in the fireplace if you make dinner," he laughed.

"Oh fuck off," I rolled my eyes walking inside and shut the door in Calebs cute, dimpled face. I seriously can't take this, what the heck were they thinking?

"I'm serious, you can make dinner and I'll go out and kill a big ass bear," he claimed.

I started walking up the stairs towards the bedroom, "A bear? Really? I bet a bear would be so disappointed and run far away from you," I commented, strolling towards the bathroom since I needed to pee.

"Aww why are you so mean to me?" He hollered while walking up the steps to the bedroom.

"Because you're annoying!" I shouted from behind the door, "but it's why you love me," he said peering his head inside the bathroom while I'm peeing.

I grabbed the pre-rolled towel and tossed it at his face, "PRIVACY ARES! GOD!"

"You really shouldn't call on God like that unless you're praying," he laughed ignoring my attempt to get him to stop looking inside while I'm PEEING!

I shot him a stern glare, "I'm going to murder you when I get out of this bathroom," I hissed.

"Don't get up to quick or piss will run down your leg," he grinned like a little ass kid.

"THASSIT I'M KICKING YOUR ASS!" I shouted, "Don't forget to wipe!" He claimed slamming the door shut.

I wiped, flushed, and decided to wash my hands anyways.

Oooo I swear he drives me INSANE.

I opened the door with so much force it hit the brick wall, "OH SHIT!" He shouted and I chased him around the house.

"I'M GONNA KILL YOU!" I shouted, trying not to be out of breath, "Hold it gorgeous, you'll mess up your hair," he laughed to make fun of me, dipping behind the marbled island counter in the open style kitchen.

I forget he trains in martial arts and is fast, I thought as he ran towards the living room.

"When it comes to you, to hell with my hair," I argued while chasing him behind the couch.

I grabbed a pillow and tossed it at his back.

But he dodged it like dodge ball, "Missed!" He grinned.

"How the hell did you not get your face scarred from pissing people off?" I panted while placing my arms on the arm rests of the sofa.

"Easy, I learned how to fight until I kept winning most of the time," he beamed while adjusting his locs.

"How about this PRINCESS, I'll go hunt and you make dinner," I huffed. He always called me Princess since I actually understood the importance of self care and at least have matching outfits. It's why girls called me boujie in high school, but whatever.

I grabbed my hair tie I kept on my wrist underneath my bracelets and tied my hair up in a bun, since it's hot down here.

"Fine with me, but good luck trying to kill a bear, I hear bears love to eat pretty girls like you," he flirted.

"Please go eat a bag of baby dicks," I cursed adjusting my hair since its sticking to the nape of my neck from how hot it is up here.

He walked towards the thermostat, "ew why baby dicks?"

"It adds insult to injury, fuck nugget," I said deciding to plop down on the couch to take my wedge sandals off.

"I love your insults, they bring me joy," he grinned turning the A/C on and I breathed a sigh of relief when the cool air blasted my face from the vent in the ceiling, "I miss your ugly ass too," I replied.

"EXCUSE ME! My ass is beautiful just like yours is," he claimed.

"Please stop flirting with me," I ignored while strolling towards my backpack to grab my shower supplies.

"Who said I was," he chuckled.

Ares wrapped his arms around my waist to pick me up, and since he's too strong I can't escape his grip, "ARES! GET OFF OF ME!" I shouted when he slung me over his shoulder like a sack of potato's. I noticed his shoulder muscle rested comfortably on my stomach, which means he's ripped, but not like super ripped.

"THE BEAST HAS CAPTURED THE PRINCESS!! MUAHAHA!" He cackled.

The rumble from his voice made the coil in my lower abdomen wind tighter until my pussy throbbed.

How pitiful am I that I'm craving sex at a random moment like this? Seriously?? UGH!

He walked towards the kitchen with ease, I gave up fighting him.

"I'm over you and your bullshit," I mentioned.

"Aww you're no fun," he whined spanking my ass and, that is not the type of stimulation I needed. At all.

He plopped me down on the island counter and placed his hands on his hips, "now are you gonna tell me what the hell happened back there with you and Caleb?" He asked, getting straight to the point.

"None of your business," I replied looking away from him.

Cuz for some reason his dark brown eyes are messing with me, and I don't like it.

Sure he definitely got bigger in size since I hadn't seen or heard from him in maybe six months or so? I still call him my best friend for the simple fact that he does know the most about me since we were always close in high school.

He hasn't changed much.

All it took was one really bad ass whooping back in high school and something inside just snapped. I was there, I saw it. He went from being the wimpy bisexual black kid, to all of a sudden, this billy bad ass in less than twenty four hours.

Seriously the way he beat that kid was ruthless, and ended up breaking his jaw and fractured his nose. It was bloody and it was why whenever I got into shit with my classmates, or dudes in general, he always fought them for me and took a heavy interest in marital arts after that.

But I've always loved him, regardless. When I thought that my heart skipped, but I brushed the feeling aside.

We fell off when we started college, and are now on this trip, so I hadn't really talked to him since the breakup with Caleb that I never told him about.

"I know when you're hiding something from me. Listen I don't mind being cool with him for the sake of the trip, but do me a favor and stop lying to me, otherwise I will ask your mom what happened," he threatened.

"Please don't," I pleaded.

"Then please tell me what happened?"

"Well you first, what happened since you dropped off the face of the earth and never called or texted me?" I fussed crossing my arms over my chest.

Having big boobs is so annoying, cuz I always have to be aware when I squeeze them together around guys. Seriously the struggle is real.

He looked down at my chest for a quick second, smiled, the turned around, "I was busy passing my classes, getting money and hoes, why?" He said while reaching inside his bag for a bottle of liquor, "Is it really that simple for you?" I replied.

"Yeah, it's that simple for me, ain't no one gonna love me, so I might as well love me more than other people try to," he replied.

Then reached for short glasses in the cabinet to pour me a shot of tequila.

I sighed when I noticed he pulled out my favorite bottle of tequila to pour in shot glasses and got the rest of the stuff ready for us to take shots.

It's annoying how well he knows me.

"Try to?" I asked.

My phone rang and it was a text from Pheebs letting me know to meet outside for a bonfire party later tonight.

"Yeah babes, try to, which translation means, until people love themselves, ain't no one gonna love me like I do, so I say fuck it and live life," he mentioned while getting the salt and lime ready for our shots.

"Must be nice," I commented shaking my head.

Ares gave me the shot, and the lime in the other hand, as I offered the back of my hand that held the lime for him to pour the salt. We have a way of moving in sync regardless of how much time has passed. It's just how we are.

"Not really, it's a choice love, and I choose to live this way, thatssit," he paused raising his glass to me, "cheers baby cakes, I missed you," he smirked.

My heart jumped to my throat when he called me love, and the longer we hang out like old times, I realized how much I did miss him.

At the same time, we clinked glasses, licked the salt, took the shot, and bit into the lime.

Damn I forgot how good this shit is.

"Yeah Imma be fucked up by the time I make it to the party tonight," I told him.

"Good, you need to smile more," he said tickling under my arm pits like a weirdo, I laughed and snorted, "STAHP!"

"NEVER!" He laughed like an evil villain.

Yeah, I missed my little shit.

Chapter 3: My Real Best Friend Or?
Yumi

"You remember how you ball tapped Jamie and then ran off like a little pussy and then blamed ME for it!" Ares laughed so hard until he turned red in the face while rolling on the floor of the cozy living room.

Black guys do turn colors, you just can't see it like I can.

I laughed so hard, I coughed, "YOU WERE NOT SUPPOSED TO REMEMBER THAT!"

"OR when ya ass made out with Jessica at Sarah's party out of no where," he said pouring another shot, "I hate you so much I swear I do," I cackled.

"Nah real shit, I heard you turned her lesbo after that make out session," Ares coughed from laughing so hard.

"Shut the fuck uuuup!" I said swatting his shoulder, "don't get me started on your shit!" I slurred.

"Like what Princess?" He beamed offering me a shot, "uh, remember how you literally told Henry that you could suck his dick better than his girlfriend all because you wanted to?" I said deciding to take the final shot and set it down on the glass coffee table.

"Yeah, cuz who gonna stop me?" He raised a cocky eyebrow and took another shot.

Damn, I can't keep up with him anymore, since when did he learn to drink me under the table? I think we had been drinking for like an hour or so? I lost track of time. I don't ever really check my phone as much when we hangout.

"GAWD you're such an arrogant asshole!" I snorted a laugh.

There was a knock at the door and when I sat up from the rug, I stumbled.

Ares caught me before I fell by grabbing my waist, "Whoa easy there, don't need you busting your ass cuz I'll end up paying for it," he reminded.

"Oh kiss my dick Ares," I slurred.

"I would if you had one."

"Please stop," I couldn't stop smiling, but the room is spinning the longer I'm standing up. Not good.

I'm not one of those girls that doesn't know when I have to puke. It's why no one ever got a photo of me vomiting. I'm too pretty for that.

"Take me to the bathroom before you answer the door," I commented and swallowed the bile rising in my throat. Please stay down, the last thing I want is to ruin a really cute outfit.

"Got it," he stated lifting me in his arms bridal style, "Ay! Pheebs, we'll be there in a lil bit!" He shouted to the door while walking me up the steps.

"Ugh, fine!" She whined.

I clutched him by the nape and tucked my head to his chest; damn, he smells good I thought licking the crevice of his neck and nibbled, giggling.

"Mm, goddammit Yumi, you're drunk," he groaned.

"Yup, and horny," I admitted.

"I don't need to know that."

"You smell good," I giggled.

"Please stop."

"Why?" I asked.

"Because I WILL fuck you and then feel bad about it later," he said honestly.

He kicked the door open like captain caveman and I just giggled some more.

Which now that I think about it, he is really masculine for a bisexual dude.

He set me down, lifted the seat, and held my hair away from my face. So when nothing came up, he stuck his finger down my throat, until I vomited in the toilet.

Ew, so gross.

"There ya go," he said rubbing my back, and I threw up some more.

"Feel better?" He asked tying my hair away and tore off some toilet paper to wipe my lips, "I hate you," I groaned as he wiped.

"No you don't, and you know it," he winked.

He washed his hands, flushed the toilet for me and went to grab me a bottle of water.

Yeah no more drinking for the night, I thought as I leaned against the jacuzzi style tub, hoping the cold porcelain would stop the throbbing in the back of my head.

I closed my eyes since the lights hurt.

Then I felt the bottle in my hand, so I twisted the cap and took a sip.

"Drink all of it if you wanna go to the bon fire party," he argued.

"Aww come on," I whined through closed eyes.

"Yumi," he got firm with me and the base in his voice is not what I'm used to, so I did. Which only made my head hurt worse.

"I'm not going," I complained.

"Yeah you are, come on, stand up," he commented.

I did and didn't stumble which is a good sign. Then while I was brushing my teeth, he spanked my ass and I shot him a hard glare, "ARES NOT NOW!"

"Yeah you're okay," he laughed then shut the door behind. The toothbrush dangled from my mouth and I looked at myself. Damn, I look rough.

I can't let Caleb see me like this. I won't.

So I took a quick shower, he got me clothes to wear and when I finished, I asked if he could help me look decent before going. So he helped me with my makeup and I combed & curled my hair with a curling iron.

"Better?" I asked, "you don't look like a gremlin if that's what you're asking me," he joked.

I shot him a blank glare, "I'll take that as a yes," I rolled my eyes.

Both of us gathered our stuff and walked out the front door to join the party.

I decided on timberland boots, shorts and a long sleeve crop top since it was cool outside and not chilly.

"HEY!" Pheebs shouted bolting to us and wrapped her arms around Ares, "Well look at you gorgeous, you clean up nicely," he grinned.

"Why are you always so rude? Can't you be nice for once?"

"I was being nice," he reminded.

"Pheebs just ignore him," I instructed and avoided eye contact with Caleb who was walking towards me from the bonfire, "hey, what took you guys so long? We missed you two," Caleb smiled attempting to be friendly.

"Oh we were fuckin in the shower," he told Caleb and the blood drained from my face, "YUMI!!" Pheebs replief with a shocked expression.

"WE WERE NOT!" I fussed.

"Oh you should've heard her, she came like, twice, maybe three times?" He claimed with confidence.

Calebs expression dropped all together, "Dude thats not possible for a girl to cum that many times in the shower, if at all. Everyone knows shower sex is fuckin terrible," Caleb challenged, folding his arms across his chest.

"I bet I can out fuck you," Ares slurred with a smirk.

"WE DID NOT FUCK!" I blushed.

"Kidding, she's right we didn't," Ares said attempting to clear the confusion, but, the look on Calebs face did not sit right with me; cuz he looked MAD. Like furious.

The last time I saw him that mad was when his dad refused to pay his credit card bill.

Wait, was that why Ares said it? To see if he was jealous?

"Ares! You play too much!" Pheebs frowned while stomping back to the campfire and Caleb followed behind her, saying nothing to either us.

"ARES!" I shouted while marching towards the rest of them, "he still wants you, cuz he got mad mad," he whispered in my ear.

"I hate you," I replied, "and stop it!" I swatted at him.

"Come stop me hoe," he joked pinching the skin of my lower back, "ARES!" I hollered.

"You called?" He said cooly sitting in the chair in front of the fire and put the bottle of tequila next to him.

"Bro you're totally sloshed," Caleb laughed, "Sure as shit am," Ares smiled.

I sat in between Pheebs and Ares, then fixed my hair, deciding now would be a good time to check my phone and see if I got a text from my mom, and nothing.

So I figured I might as well send her the smoke signal.

"Mom, I'm drunk, I just puked, I'm sharing a room with Ares instead because Pheebs tried to set me up with Caleb in a one bedroom cabin, and Ares looks sexy. Help," I texted.

"Oh, my poor baby, does Ares still look as good as I remember? I knew he would be a looker when he got older."

"MOM! YOU'RE NOT HELPING!" I texted back with crying emoji's at the end.

"And yes, yes he does. He got more muscly," I texted ending with the drooling emoji.

"Ooo, so why not smash? You're young, and he cares about you, unlike bitch ass Caleb," my mom sent back.

Pheebs turned on some music and it was one of my favorite Kpop songs by Kara "Wanna."

"MOM!! We're friends, NO!"

And my mom didn't text back for a minute, only to have my phone ring with an instagram photo she sent me of him.

I glared at the photo and the heat rose to my cheeks the longer I stared at it.

"Sis, seriously?? Smash him FOR ME!" My mom replied with crying emojis.

I love my mom.

But shes not kidding, he does look REALLY good. When did he get tattoos!!!

And yeah he fits the usual image; the tall, dark skinned, muscly black guy, with only a few tattoos and purple locs.

He was shirtless wearing a weed hat that covered his eyes with a sexy smirk.

Why is my heart racing the longer I look at him? And why are all of the memories I have of us coming to the surface right now?

Like the time I held him in my arms when his mom called the cops on him. Or the time he tried to teach me how to twerk. The many times we would smoke in my car and talk about life and shit.

Those were the moments he was so sexy to me, I thought with a smile on my lips.

Then a pang hit my chest, but—we can't.

We're friends.

Right?

"Want to dance?" Caleb asked breaking me from my thoughts, "Uh, yeah sure," I agreed not thinking about my answer since I'm still kinda buzzed.

Shit.

I looked up and noticed Ares dancing with Pheebs and then decided to twerk, because he can, and the fact that I can see what his butt looks like under his cargo shorts, is not an image I needed.

Why DOES his butt look better than mine?? I thought as he fell into the music, lip syncing the song with her.

I took Calebs hand and he pulled me closer by the waist to close the distance between us. Our eyes met and the last time he kissed me flashed in my mind.

I blushed and turned away from him because my heart wouldn't stop racing the longer he looked down at me.

Then the song switched to Christina Aguilera Your Body.

Crap.

"Can we talk?" He asked.

"We are talking," I replied peering over his shoulder only to see Pheebs sitting down checking her phone while Ares was dancing.

His plaid button down shirt was completely open while he swayed his hips to the music. Just lost to his own world.

The fluidity of his movements held a masculine air about him that should not exist.

How the hell does he do that? And why does he look good doing it? Goober.

"You've been staring at him the whole night Yumi," Caleb whispered.

He pressed me against him and I snapped my head to face him, "So what?" I snapped.

"We need more boys," Ares announced out of no where, but kept doing his thing.

"No Ares we do not, I can't deal with too much testosterone as is," Pheebs replied.

"Aww come on! Take another shot, you're too uptight!" He joked sitting in her lap and she fought with him, "STOP IT!" She argued.

"So you just won't listen to anything I have to say will you?" Caleb snarled.

"What for? You're getting married Caleb, what more is there to talk about?!" I declared.

I broke his grip and stomped away from him, while trying not to let my tears reach the brim. I needed to walk further away from Ares and Pheebs right now, I don't want them to hear what we're talking about.

"So what? You know it's just a business transaction!" He replied chasing behind me.

"So what?! That's your family, you humiliated me, by telling all those people who called me a rat, poor gutter trash, or a rube by saying NOTHING. Fuck you forever Caleb!" I argued.

"What the hell was I supposed to say in front of my FAMILY?!? In front of those people my parents made those deals with?!?" He cursed.

"Yo!" Ares shouted and the base in his voice made me jump, "the fuck you want?" Caleb growled.

"We should play a game," he said with a smirk on his lips. Wait when did he follow us?

"What?" Caleb shot him a confused glare.

I knew he was just doing it to stop me from crying again.

"Truth and Dare," he grinned.

"Uhm, isn't it Truth OR Dare?" Pheebs asked, "Nah, that shit is old. So we gonna make some shit up and make it fun, you down Pheebs? Even though I know ya ass is always gonna pick truth, which is why its called Truth AND Dare," Ares joked.

"No fair!" Pheebs whined and he lifted her bridal style, "No take backs, besides the crew is finally all together again! So lets do what we came to do," Ares said as Pheebs accidentally kicked Caleb in his back, "And thats party bitches!" He laughed spinning Pheebs around.

"OW DAMMIT PHOEBE!" Caleb shouted and I laughed.

"PUT ME DOWN!" She shouted but I saw her smile.

Yeah everyone loves Ares. I guess that's the other reason I can add to the list.

Caleb frowned, and looked at me, "you like him don't you?" He asked me out of no where, "What?" I said.

"It's written all over your face, you never loved me. Whatever, I guess my family was right about you, and I dodged a bullet. They were right to call you a gold digger," he said coldly. His words cut me like a knife and I couldn't breathe for a moment.

"Sure! What's the rules?" Caleb asked while returning to his original friendly demeanor.

I dry swallowed the lump in my throat, "asshole," I choked back my tears under my breath.

I turned around and took a deep breath, "I'm strong, I'm strong, I'm strong," I whispered to myself so I could stop myself from crying in front of everyone.

No one will ever know what he just said to me, and I'll bury it like I do everything else.

With one final breath shoving it down, I turned around and sat down, "What's the rules?"

Ares eyed me from over the flame and I blinked cuz I've only seen that expression from him when he was about to beat someone's ass. It made my stomach clench and the hairs on the back of my neck stand up, because somehow it looked darker than I remember.

But he broke into a smile, "So here's how it works; I say Yumi, Truth, then ask a question. She answers, then she picks either truth or dare for the next person say she tells Caleb Dare and has to do the dare. Now if he backs out of Dare, someone else gets to dictate his punishment. And the same goes for Truth. Simple punishments like drinking, loss of money, paying for something, shit like that," he explained rolling up a blunt.

"Sounds like fun, I'm game," Caleb agreed.

I tried not to panic, this does not sound like a good idea with what just happened between me and Caleb. Not right now.

Ares what the hell are you doing?

"Does anyone get to be a fact checker in this?" Pheebs asked, "you know if someone is lying and we can call them out on the lie," she said to Ares looking up from her phone screen.

"Ooo I like that addition, I dictate that role to the ladies then," he responded cheerfully.

"Yeah since women are good liars, they would be able to know when someone is telling the truth, huh yeah right," Caleb laughed grabbing his beer and sipped it.

"Caleb! That's not nice," She said with a frown.

"Now THAT is the truth," Caleb slurred a laugh.

"You guys ready? I'll go first," Ares paused, slouched in his chair and shot Caleb the most evil glare I had ever seen from him.

"Caleb, Truth."

Chapter 4: Truth & Dare

Yumi

"What did you say to Yumi a few seconds ago before we decided to play," Ares slouched in his chair with the lit blunt hanging from his lips, thighs spread apart and a menacing glare.

The air suddenly got tense, and Caleb chuckled taking another sip of his beer.

"I said she's lucky to have dated me, and not you," he said swirling the beer in the glass bottle.

"Oh no," I heard Pheebs whisper.

Ares tilted his head and blew the smoke out of nose, "Yumi, is that what he said?" He asked calmly.

Too calmly and it's why my heart is racing and plummeting to the pits at the same time.

"Guys I don't want fights," Pheebs pleaded sensing the tension between the two of them the longer they glared at each other, over me.

"Nah we good," he reassured with an all knowing smirk, blowing more smoke out of his nose.

"Yeah thats what he said," I rolled my eyes.

"Yumi, Truth, did you fuck Ares while we were together?" Caleb asked me outright.

I think I choked on my spit when he said it and I started coughing, "Are you fucking kidding me??" I slipped.

"Guys WHY are these questions about SEX?!" Pheebs groaned in agitation.

"Cuz sex is awesome," Ares answered.

"I am so tired of you guys! Ugh!" She fussed.

Then gulped her beer like a frat girl, which is really not like her, what's going on with Pheebs, I've never seen her like this before?

"THERE! Now I'm not left behind like you guys keep trying to do with me every time we used to do this kinda stuff together," she argued folding her arms across her chest.

"No Caleb I didn't," but the more he mentions it, I should have years ago like I wanted to back then, and it really made me wonder if we could be together like that.

"Nah, we didn't," Ares confirmed, taking one more puff and passed the blunt to Caleb, "yet," flashing a cocky smirk.

"I mean really Caleb, you're so cute," Ares mocked, just to piss him off.

I know when he's doing things to make other people upset, fighting my battles for me like he always did.

It made my chest ache and wanna throw up altogether.

Or maybe I'm just fucked up from drinking earlier?

Caleb rolled his eyes, took the blunt from him, inhaled, and coughed.

It was my turn now.

"Pheebs, dare," I said but she cut me off before I had a chance to finish.

"WHAT!" She snapped.

"Hey, you okay?" I asked, worried cuz shes really out of character right now.

"You guys really think arranging all of this was easy?? And then you bring up all this stupid crap that does not matter! We came out here to have fun! And not fight! On top of it, I know you're gonna ask me to dare and do something I normally wouldn't want to do, so just come on and get it over with," she complained.

I've never seen her like this. Ever.

I stood up from my chair and sat beside her, "You don't have to play if you don't want to," I reminded.

"I'm so tired of being left behind," she whispered only to me.

I get it, we have been assholes to her while needing her at the same time, but she's always been the one to keep our asses in line and I love her for it.

I wouldn't want her to change unless she wants to, cuz it's not worth losing someone else I love and care for, it never is.

"hey, don't mind us, we're just being stupid," Ares chimed as his way of comforting her. It made me smile as I rubbed her back to comfort her.

"But I always feel like such a little kid, I've only had one boyfriend, I'm not like all of you," she pouted.

"Okay I'll change it, Pheebs, Truth, if there is one thing you could do, anything in the entire world, what would it be?" I asked instead.

"I wanna run outside naked!" she exclaimed with her eyes closed. She's so adorable.

All of us glared at her and Ares coughed as if he didn't hear her correctly.

"I need another beer, pass me that blunt!" She said grabbing it from Caleb and took a hit. Coughed, and groaned.

Then flashed me a really warm smile, as if proud of herself for doing something I knew she always wanted to do, "I did it didn't I?" She said.

"You're a real G," I reassured.

But it's my job at her bestie to make sure she was doing it for the right reasons and not because of us.

"You okay?" I said to be sure.

"Yeah, cuz I've always wanted to do that, honestly, sorry I got irritated with you," she apologized.

"Wanna go running naked together? On some totally non sexual shit? I love streaking," Ares offered.

Pheebs took her jacket and tossed it at him, "NO!" She giggled.

"Better with me than alone, Jussayin," he laughed.

"How do you put with him?" Pheebs asked offering me the blunt, "I have no idea," I replied.

She looked down in her lap, "thanks for having my back Yumi, and sorry for that random outburst," she replied sincerely.

"You have no idea how long I was waiting for that from you, cuz I knew it was always in there, I'm proud of you, how do you feel?" I inquired.

"Fuckin awesome," she finally cursed.

"HOOPLAH!" Ares shouted as if celebrating her first curse word.

"You're such a terrible influence," I joked walking back to my chair, "I know," he replied with that same cheesy grin.

"But we love you," Pheebs replied with a dorky grin on her lips towards Ares.

"Dawwww I love you too pumpkin!" He said randomly getting up and kissing her cheek, "EW GET OFF OF MEEE!" She laughed.

It warmed my heart to see my friends like this, and for once to see Phoebe having fun.

She was always the coordinator and always spent more time in her phone than participating.

So to see her smiling was exactly what she needed.

Thanks Ares, I thought to myself taking another hit of the blunt.

The sounds of the forest increased in volume, and I smiled at the buzz.

Shit, I'm fucked up.

I sat back down in my chair and waited for Pheebs to pick someone.

"Okay! I'm gonna try something a little different guys is that okay?" She asked to be sure.

"Go 'head gurl," Ares encouraged as I passed the blunt to him.

"Yumi, truth, what did Caleb REALLY say?" She called me out.

The blood drained from my face.

Goddammit, why Pheebs? After the moment we just had??

Caleb shot me a stern glare as if to tell me don't answer that, and it pissed me off.

I covered and defended him the first time, but the fact he's getting married and hasn't said shit to anyone, while thinking he can tell me what I can and can't do, even in this situation, is infuriating.

I sighed, "He said that his family was right to call me a gold digger," I admitted.

Ares just licked his lips and laughed.

"Ohhh so you think cuz you got money you better than everyone, aiight, good to know," Ares said, raising the bottle to him, "Cheers to you bruh, you take the cake on knowing how to hurt the only one whose had your back since day one," He reminded.

"What the fuck would you know?!" Caleb argued, "Cuz I was there," Ares snickered just to mock him.

"Caleb why would you say something so awful to Yumi!" Pheebs finally called him out.

Guys stop. I don't want fighting.

"Cuz its true, she decided to go out with me once I started bitching about how hard it was being a rich kid back then, but she didn't ask me before, and pursued me like a lost puppy," he insulted.

I grit my teeth and swallowed my tears.

"CALEB!" Phoebe stomped to him with balled fists.

Ares just laughed, "wow bruh you got your shit all fucked up, what bitch told you that lie?" He mentioned.

"Otherwise why stalk me like she did back then? She had her sights set on me since the beginning and was just—" Caleb started to say but Phoebe slugged him, hard.

Wait! What the hell is HAPPENING!

"How dare you say such awful things! The reason she was stalking you was because you were SUICIDAL and was worried about you! As far as targeting you, she never did that on purpose! She's a good person who actually loved you! You were FRIENDS!" Phoebe reminded with trembling hands.

Ares gently touched her shoulders to calm her down, "don't worry Imma kick his ass later, hows your hand?" He reassured calmly.

"Yumi aren't you going to say anything?!" Pheebs demanded to know why I wasn't bothered with it, or him.

"No, however he views me is how he sees it," I answered with a defeated tone.

"Ugh whatever," Caleb said holding his cheek while glaring hard at Phoebe.

Ares shot him a death glare, "hit her and I will murder you," he hissed.

The cold rumble in his tone made me shiver and my blood pulse hot at the same time.

"I know not to hit a woman," Caleb hissed sipping another beer.

"Now lets be adults about this," Ares said calmly, "Caleb do you need a break or would you like to go to your room?" He continued to make fun of as if he couldn't handle being hit in the face and needed a time out.

"Nah, I'm good," he replied, "Ohh tough guy, I like that," he winked.

Everyone took their seats and now its my turn to pick someone, and to be honest, I'm too sloshed, and angry at everything.

I figured now would be a good time to support all of Ares attempts to piss off Caleb.

"Ares dare," I said. Hoping he would follow me on what I was about to ask. Because this is what could make or break our friendship.

"Finally!" He beamed.

"Kiss me," I said locking my eyes with him over the fire.

I looked over at Caleb and he looked pissed, and hurt.

Good. Serves his ass right.

"Ooooo," Phoebe said taking the blunt from Ares and took another hit.

"Ain't gotta tell me twice baby," he sprung to his feet.

Then crouching to me, our eyes met and my heart thumped loudly against my chest. Looking at him made me wanna cry and break down in his arms again, but I can't right now.

He cupped my cheek in his palm, "I gotchu," he whispered to let me know he knew why I asked him to kiss me and wasn't upset with me. He's—matured since then. I see it now.

I swallowed my spit, and hoped my breath didn't smell bad, but, looking in his eyes and tuning out the world, I honestly didn't care. It was just us like it always had been, right Ares?

He slowly pulled me towards him, and when our lips met in the center, he ignited me like a depraved beast, yearning to taste more of him.

Ares I can't hear anything, just my heart beating in my ears. I want more, I know I do.

I ran the tips of my fingers in his locs and chasing my impulse, I parted my mouth to meet his tongue in the center, with the sole need to devour him.

His vulnerable groan in my mouth made me shiver and I clasped his hair in my palms, while his hands cupped my cheeks like I was someone he cherished more than anyone.

I don't care if my lipgloss is smudging, I don't care that his breath tastes like weed and tequila, I don't care how I look, just know that I can't breathe the deeper I'm kissing him right now.

He matched his needs with mine in the center with the same intensity and we both purred in each other's mouth. God I want him. I can't lie anymore. Please don't have this moment break our friendship, okay?

He broke from my lips, and pulled away from me. Our eyes met I couldn't help but let the tears rise to the brim, knowing I needed to cry, but only to him and no one else.

Ares expression was so tender when he just shook his head no, as if to say 'please don't cry'

He knows how I feel about crying in front of others and—I love him so much for it.

"Sorry," I apologized with a slight nod blinking my tears away.

He grabbed me and tenderly kissed my temple lingering for another moment before returning to his chair. Ending our intimate moment just as quick as it started.

I blushed and looked away from everyone, deciding now would be a good time to try and regather myself by fixing my lipgloss again.

"Well now that that's done, it's my turn isn't it?" Ares claimed, reaching for the blunt from Caleb who refused to pass it.

He took another hit before giving it back.

"Hm, Pheebs, Truth, was that the first time you punched someone or have you done anything violent before?"

"I stabbed a girl with a pencil in second grade, she got lead poisoning and I ended up getting suspended from school because of it," she admitted shyly.

Ares offered me the last of the blunt, but I knew to say no, because as high as I am, I will fuck him out here in the woods.

"Daaaaaaaaamn you're a bad ass," He said.

"Not really, my mom called me a monster because of it," she said somberly.

"Well thats cuz we all know your mom is a—" He started but Pheebs cut him off.

"Ares! Don't!"

"My bad, ya'll know I got a shitty family," he replied nonchalantly.

"Well it's my turn isn't it?" Phoebe said turning her attention back to Caleb's salty expression.

"Caleb, Truth, Did you ever really love anyone? Other than yourself?" She asked wryly.

I've NEVER seen her like this. Like ever.

"Yeah, and it was my ex," he rolled his eyes.

"I call bullshit," Ares chimed.

"You know I was rooting for you Caleb, until you said that awful thing about her," Phoebe claimed.

We're all fucked up, I can tell by the way were all slouching and shit. Especially Ares since we were drinking before we got here.

"Really?" He said confused while still holding his cheek.

Yeah thats gonna leave a bruise.

"Yes! I thought you guys had some falling out but nothing that awful and spiteful," she said as if she was bothered by it more than me.

I'm so over people fighting my battles for me, so I decided to come out with why we really broke up.

"It was a party I went to and he's engaged as a business deal," I announced, and my gaze fell to my lap, "and he didn't tell me until the day of the ball, and thats why you found me that way when I called you Ares. I'm sorry, I just didn't want to burden you with my shit anymore," I admitted.

"My family blackmailed me Yumi! They said they would make you an OnlyFans page and post all the naked photos YOU sent me when we were together if I didn't get married to her!" Caleb shouted.

My heart plummeted to the pits & I think I'm gonna be sick.

"Fuck all of you!" He hollered standing up and stormed off into the the woods.

We all just sat there stunned and now I realize my heart can't take much more of this shit. It can't.

So which is the truth? That I'm a gold digger, or that his family black mailed me?

"So I'm inclined to beat both of their asses, dually noted," Ares said as if making a mental note.

"Yumi are you okay?" Phoebe asked with concern.

I smiled, "sure why?" I replied normally.

I'm honestly too high to be upset as I normally would be sober.

"I'll go get Prince Charming," Ares commented.

He hopped from his chair and went after him, leaving me and Phoebe alone.

I'm sure blows will be exchanged at some point, because I know he doesn't like fighting in front of me if he can avoid it.

"You're not okay," Phoebe affirmed.

"I know, but I'm too high to care."

"Well now isn't this a mess," she frowned and I knew she was beating herself up thinking it was her fault, and its not.

"Hey Pheebs, its fine, it's not your fault.

"I didn't know, why didn't you say anything to me?" She said teary eyed.

"You know how I am Pheebs, I didn't wanna bother anyone," I replied. I didn't want her to cry.

"But Ares knew!"

"No, he didn't know what happened. Both of you are just finding out, and I'm just now finding out what Caleb wanted to tell me this entire time," I said out loud.

"Still, his family called you shitty things, and you shouldn't take him back. Especially if I don't approve," she frowned and crossed her arms, "he's not worthy of you."

"I know," I smiled warmly. Her disapproval reminded me of my mom and I seriously appreciated it.

"But seriously, I can tell by the way Ares looks at you, he's in love with you," she said out of no where.

I paled, "what?"

"You couldn't tell?" She said stunned, like I missed something.

"Nooo thats not like him," I refuted.

"You're so dense," Pheebs huffed.

"Seriously? You couldn't tell by the way he kissed you? I could," she claimed with a giddy expression.

She decided to sit next to me and shoved her phone in my hands. The blood drained from my face; it was video of me and Ares kissing.

It was a good angle too cuz you could clearly see us both from a three quarter view. With the dark forest behind me where I sat in the chair, and him on his knees between my thighs with the fire behind him.

No I don't wanna know. I really don't wanna know.

"Please don't play that," I asked, "too late," she giggled, pressing play.

It didn't help that she had zoomed in to capture the intensity of it; both of his hands had cupped my cheeks and the tips of my fingers were in his hair, in sync and it was my first time kissing him. Ever.

In all the years we had been friends, that's the first time I've kissed him.

What's even more jarring to me, is noticing the way we kissed each other; because if I didn't think it was me kissing Ares, there was no way to refute how we feel for each other in the way our lips locked.

Then the moment when he broke from me, I had looked so vulnerable and scared.

I actually saw my lip quiver, it wasn't pretty either.

But, I could tell by his mannerisms that he was being soft and tender with me, then he kissed my temple and that was it.

I can't take much more of this emotional roller coaster. I thought that—he did it just to piss of Caleb with me? But, it did feel like more? Or maybe I'm just fucked up? I don't know anymore.

Pheebs texted me the video and my phone dinged.

"BACK!" Ares shouted.

I immediately locked my phone and put it away, "the wonder boys return," Phoebe giggled since they looked like they had been fighting.

And clearly Ares won.

BY THE TIME EVERYONE calmed down, they both told us that they did get in a fight and Pheebs shot me an all knowing glare with a smirk that said, 'see I told you so.'

I just ignored it and decided to go to my main source in confusing situations like these. So I sent the video to my mom really quick hoping she had seen it so she can help me figure this out.

"Mom? Thoughts?" I texted.

"Dear sweet Jesus, he is FINE!" With the heart eyes emojis. Lots of them.

I laughed at her text, God my mom is seriously the best. I love her so much.

"Listen here, LINDA, if you do NOT smash this man, I will hold you personally accountable for robbing me of my youthful dreams," she said with a laughing emoji.

"You aint shit," I texted with the same laughing emojis.

I did smile into my phone and tried not to cry, cuz I can hear her voice in my head as shes texting me. I won't show them my tears, not right now.

"I know, but seriously, you sure he's not in love with you? I mean men don't kiss like that, the last man that ever kissed me like that was your father. Damn was he good in bed," she admitted with crying emojis.

I ignored her last comment.

"What makes you think he's in love with me?" I asked.

Seriously, how the hell can everyone else tell BUT me??

"It's the way he's looking at you baby, men don't give just any woman THAT look. Does he look at Phoebe that way? No? Then yeah he's in love with you. Jesus your just as dense as your father, rest his soul, I miss him," she replied.

"Really?" I asked.

"Of course, I loved him and still do," she admitted. I always respected that about her, she still decided to love him through it all and it never affected my relationship with him as his daughter.

"You were always the coolest mom," I texted.

"I know baby, but seriously, how are you feeling? Call me if you need to talk cuz I can tell you sound confused and something else happened that your not telling me," she replied too quick.

Everyone calls that a mothers intuition, I call it witchcraft.

"Hey guys I'll be right back," I said grabbing a water from the plastic bag and walked off, saying nothing to anyone.

Thank God we have reception out here.

I made sure I was a good distance from the group before calling her, "Mom?"

"What happened?" She asked in her soothing mom voice.

Yup, I feel it bubbling inside, I'm about to ugly cry.

"Mom, I don't, it's just been too much stuff," I started, not sure where to begin with everything that happened.

"What did Caleb say to you?" She cut straight the chase, "he said something really hurtful, then the real reason we broke up," I said glaring up at the moon that peeked through the leaves.

"Which was?" She asked and I could tell from the hiss in her voice at his name, she really hates him.

"He said he was bribed by his family to break up with me. But that was only after Ares made a joke about us fuckin in our cabin to gauge Calebs reaction to me," I told her.

"Mhm," she replied and I kept going, "thing is, he said, his family was right to think of me as a gold digger, then told everyone that I had targeted him since the beginning. Even when we were friends," I admitted.

"FUCK HIM! AND FOR THE LOVE OF GOD FUCK ARES!" My mom practically shouted, "Oh my God Mom!"

"I'm sorry, but baby listen to me, in moments like these you have to learn how to keep tally of whose been on your side versus who hasn't. Take this situation for example, Ares told a bold faced LIE to gauge your EX boyfriends reaction to you since he KNEW he was being dishonest, or said some shady shit. Which means he's smart and trusts his own judgement about others when it comes to you and safety of YOUR emotions," she explained.

"Well he did ask Caleb outright what he said that made me almost break down in front of everyone in the middle of Truth and Dare," I admitted.

"See he didn't pussy around the topic, played his cards right, and kissed you to probably make him jealous to back YOU up. Gurl don't you know that man is in love with you?" She said like it was obvious.

"How can you know that mom? I haven't seen him in half a year," I admitted and my chest ached when I thought about it.

"And he probably missed you, you know they say absence makes the heart grow fonder," she mentioned.

"Mom, are you sure?" I asked, unsure of what's going on right now. Just because I'm an adult does not mean I got this shit figured out. At all.

"How do you feel about it?" She comforted.

"I mean, you're right, he has had my back the whole time since this trip started. He offered to stay in the cabin with me instead of Caleb cuz he knew I didn't want to be bothered with it. Then we drank together, laughed a lot, and he even held my hair when I threw up. Then everything else I told you that happened at the bonfire. Ares made Caleb mad by saying random stuff, then Caleb got pissed with him but Ares didn't fight him cuz I asked him not to. So he still respected my needs. And I didn't have to say anything to Ares when I dared him to kiss me, he knew I wanted to piss him off, and—" I couldn't keep going cuz my chest feels tight at the weight of what my mom said to me.

"Mhm, the man loves you, just be honest with yourself and him, cuz he's done the same for you, so please don't be like me and do fuck girl shit like I did when I was your age," she reminded.

"I do love him, but I just don't know if it's in love with him," I said, not sure if I wanted to admit to myself why out loud.

I don't want to lose my best friend.

"Think of it this way, can you imagine spending another day without him? And I'm not talking about he stops talking and moves on in life, I mean like how your father died in a car accident, fatal. I hate to make it so serious, but that's really the only way we can know the truth of our feelings, cuz we all like to think we can live without someone until they aren't here anymore, permanently," she explained.

I get why she felt the need to do that, but she's right.

I can't. So then what about, Caleb? I couldn't imagine the thought without him in the picture alive either.

God this shit is tearing me apart!

"Be honest with yourself," my mom warned.

Witch.

"Thing is, I thought for a long time I couldn't live without Caleb. There was a time I thought that, but I have no idea how I would have gotten through my breakup if it wasn't for Ares, the more I think about it. Besides, Caleb is getting married, and—" he's hurt me too many times for me to go back.

Even with knowing the truth.

I can't go back.

"How did you feel kissing him?" She asked like a giddy bestie.

"Like I couldn't breathe for a second," I slipped.

"Marry him," She said out of no where.

"MOM!" I whined.

"Besides, I wouldn't mind having him as a son in law," she said like she was purring.

Dear God, thank you for blessing me with this amazing woman. Amen.

"I'm hanging up now," I laughed, "I'm serious, just think about being with him. I know he'll treat you right," she switched back to mom mode.

"Okay, I will, thanks mom," I replied covering my mouth to stop myself from crying.

"Oh and if you do smash I want all the details," she interrupted.

"BYE MOM!" I stated, giggling.

"Love you sweetheart, see you when you get back."

"Love you too," I said hanging up.

I decided to sit outside and glare at the moon for a minute alone, I needed it to sort through everything.

The worst part was, every time I did close my eyes; Ares was all I could see, his lips were all I could feel on mine and even the way he touched me like I was so precious to him. Like nothing could ever happen to me.

This is the thing that sucks about being high and slightly drunk, everything makes sense, and sometimes I wish it didn't.

Why can't I be normal like everyone else who just doesn't know?

"Miss me," Ares whispered in my ear and I jolted, "Goddammit Ares!" I swatted instinctively and covered my face, "please go away," I whined.

"You're not okay," he reminded.

"I know, I'm not."

"So?"

"So what?" I snapped, knowing I wanted to argue with him, "Oh you wanna pick a fight, bet," he replied sitting beside me and said nothing.

Literally nothing.

I sighed after a few moments and he took that as his cue to talk, "did I make shit worse? I know I'm famous for making shit worse," he mentioned.

"Yes and no," I said honestly.

"Which parts?" He asked.

"Kissing me has me confused, and I've had two people tell me that you're in love with me," I said outright.

I raised my head and gazed at him, "Truth, are you in love with me?" I asked looking into his eyes.

He didn't look shocked like I thought he would, he just smiled sweetly, "damn that obvious?" He said casually.

My heart leapt to my throat, "what?" I choked trying not to cry again.

"Yeah its true, I'm in love with you, but I didn't wanna ruin our friendship unless you were ready to take that step, and if you wanted to be just friends, I'm fine with that. I'm happy either way," he said honestly with a somber smile on his lips.

Tears fell against my will, and I shoved him, "God you're so fucking annoying," I sobbed.

"You don't have to answer, it's fine," he said wrapping his arms around and tucked me to his chest to shield me away.

"I hate you," I said, curling in a ball and sobbed harder, "I love you too Yumi," he whispered kissing the top of my head.

"And you know you sound ugly when you cry," he reminded.

"Fuck off," I whined.

"I'd fuck you till my dick stops working."

"That's not possible for you," I smiled against my will cuz he always says stupid shit to make me smile. Idiot.

"I'm down if you wanna find out," he joked, "maybe," I said with a small smile at the thought.

He tensed, "wait—what?" He said looking at me and wiped my tears, "maybe what?" He asked again wiping my snot with the end of his shirt that smeared my makeup.

But I don't care, he's seen me at my worst moments and my best moments. He's always been there. Always.

"Will you, uh, kiss me again?" I asked.

"Why?" He asked confused.

"Ares, I know I love you, but," I missed him, I missed talking with him, I missed him driving me insane, I missed him reminding me to do shit, I missed his good morning texts, I miss our long intellectual conversations, I missed his larger than life personality, I miss reminding him not to fight too much, I missed him. I even missed our fights.

"You wanna know for sure, yeah?" He smiled but it was sad.

"Please?" I asked more vulnerable than I had intended.

He nodded, and when he cupped my cheeks in his hands again, I closed my eyes and waited for our lips to meet in the center. The warmth of his lips against mine melted my flesh and made my chest explode, I forgot to breathe when our tongues met in the middle. My heart is soaring, the longer I kiss him.

Every possible memory I had shared with him assaulted the forefront of my mind and I clutched his hair in my hands, I need him. Don't leave me again.

I—

Love you.

I'm—

In love with you.

Crap. When did that happen?

When did he take my heart away from me?

I remember now, it was when he got in that fight with his mother. She had called the cops on him, and my mom backed him up. He stayed in the other room, but we stayed up that night drinking and it was the first time I had ever seen his strength.

He only shed a few tears, drank, and stared into the darkness of the guest bedroom. So I did the same, and tried to make him smile like he does with me. I held him in my lap and it was then I fell in love with him at the lowest moment of his life.

I was there for all of it. He was there for all of it.

How long did Phoebe know? How long was Caleb threatened by him? How many times did Ares swallow his pride and emotions for me? To protect me? I can tell by the way he's kissing me because I'm not breathing. I'm not here anymore. I want him, and I know it.

Mom, did you know too?

"I'm so sorry," I apologized in his lips, "for what?" He asked rubbing his thumb against my cheek, "for not knowing sooner," I cried out.

"You're dense, we all know that about you," he answered warmly.

"Shut up," I whined.

"Can I be selfish and tell you?" He asked as our eyes locked, "I love you Yumi," he replied.

The weight of his words hit me like a tidal wave, because it was firm. Like a statement with no hesitation in it. Like he knew he would give his life for me.

I knew when he said it right then, I would do the same.

"I love you too Ares, I'm sorry I didn't know sooner," I answered with more tears falling.

He blinked with shock, "What?" He paused, "did you say?"

"I love you Ares, I'm sorry I didn't know sooner, I'm an asshole, and you're right I'm super slow, hell everyone knows it," I replied laughing while crying.

The weight of confusion that was inside of my chest was lifted as soon as I said it. This, feels right.

He grinned but I knew he was trying to fight from crying, "Ah, shit, now you gonna have me crying like you and shit," he fussed.

"I'm serious, I love you Ares," I said with a smile.

"Please, say it one more time," he said tenderly.

"I love you Ares."

"One more time," he said finally as a way to joke with me and I yanked on his hair, "I love YOU Ares," I laughed, "fuck nugget," I insulted.

He kissed me again and it was passionate, needy, and his lips told me how lonely he had been without me, the part of him he spent so long trying to hide, and I can sense it now. I laid against the dewy grass and his lips hovered over mine.

"I'm in love with you Yumi, I knew I loved you since high school," he said tucking a piece of my hair behind my ear.

"Well I'm love with you," I replied, "you're still annoying."

"And you're still my beautiful little gremlin," he whispered in my lips.

"Life with you is gonna be us constantly fighting and fucking isn't it?"

He smirked, "When I'm not working, studying, or training, yes," he agreed.

"You're still making dinner though like a good wife," he teased biting my bottom lip and ran away.

"HEY! GET BACK HERE!" I shouted sitting up to chase after him.

WE MADE LOVE THAT NIGHT for the first time, and it was the first time I felt cherished, loved, needed and wanted for all of me and not just parts of me.

I had no idea we would be this sexually compatible, and he wasn't bragging when he said I would climax more than once.

And he's got stamina for years which makes this more enjoyable for me. It's a side of myself I can explore with him, and its fun actually.

I collapsed on his chest and smiled, "Mine now," he growled sinking his teeth in my neck and I moaned, "Ares STAHP!" I whined.

"I just wanted you to know who you belong to is all" he reminded.

"GOODNIGHT ARES!" I said turning over but it didn't work, cuz he tickled me, "Okay okay! I yield! Damn!" I giggled.

"Kidding," he said kissing the crevice of my neck, "night babe, I love you,"

"I love you too," I said with the widest grin on my lips.

Thank you for giving me love, when I had no idea what it was. For loving me when I was the biggest asshole to you. For always having my back even when I didn't have yours all the time.

So lets be a team together okay?

THE END.

Don't miss out!

Visit the website below and you can sign up to receive emails whenever Kornelia Blackmore publishes a new book. There's no charge and no obligation.

https://books2read.com/r/B-A-GOZN-KBVVB

BOOKS 2 READ

Connecting independent readers to independent writers.

Did you love *Truth & Dare*? Then you should read *Crowning*[1] by Kornelia Blackmore!

"Dear Layla, I hope this letter finds you well, I'm not sure if you remember me, but if it helps to jog your memory, we got married by the swings at the Greenfield playground that winter I came to the states when we were kids. Dejun Amani. I wish to inform you that the vows we took that day are valid, and due to those circumstances, I require my Queen to the throne here in the land of Azaria Erelle. This is non-negotiable and would need your presence two weeks from the date of this letter at 534 Parkville Street on the roof of the building at 10 AM. Do not worry about bringing necessities as

1. https://books2read.com/u/b5oDKR

2. https://books2read.com/u/b5oDKR

all will be provided for, should you need any of your things, they will be moved to the palace, so please, just bring yourself. I look forward to seeing you. Signed, Prince Dejun Amani Heir to the Azaria Empire. The clusterfuck of emotions hit me all at one time, happiness, omg, hope, and rage all at the same time. Happy that I finally got to hear from him, even if I never admit that to a waking soul ever, oh my God, because an actual prince even remembers me (assuming he is one and this isn't some fucked up prank); and hopeful that if this shit is real I have a solution to all my problems and I never have to work a day in my life again, ever, and angry because rolling in the back of my mind was, where the fuck were you when I needed you, with anything I ever went through. Like dude, it was a fake wedding, some shit he randomly said outta nowhere, and I just went along with it; how the hell did it turn into THIS?!

Read more at www.twitter.com/kblackmore26362.

Also by Kornelia Blackmore

Crowning
The Blood Covenant: Mistrust, Division, & Murder
Truth & Dare

Watch for more at www.twitter.com/kblackmore26362.

About the Author

I started my writing journey as an angsty teenager back in 2008, and I noticed how many reviews I kept getting for the fan fictions I wrote on their website over the years. One day I was reading a Webtoon by June Purr called SubZero and intrigued with the idea of wanting to create a world but with people of color, that's what birthed Kornelia Blackmore.

Normally this is the part where I tell you I have degrees but I don't Just another really cool mini story that set me on the path in my early college years.

I failed my English composition classes (and even creative writing). Until I came across a really cool guy named Mr. D at Prince Georges Community College.

He was one of the first people to have ever made me feel like I was a writer, and even asked me "how the hell did you end up in my class?" until eventually everyone in my class was asking me for help with their writing pieces. I think that was probably the only other time in life I felt accomplished from others asking me for help, and I grew to love the experience as a means to solidify my place as an artist.

But, writing is my lifeblood, and this is the quote I live by in all of my writing projects;

"Life has enough limitations. Writing shouldn't be one of them."

This quote is how I aspire to learn the art of writing in all its different forms and genres and will continue to pursue that passion with the same dedication in everything else I do.

I would rather you guys get to know me, as me, instead of some stuffy long biography that no one ever really reads. But thank you for buying my book, and reading it.

Blessings friends.

Read more at www.twitter.com/kblackmore26362.

About the Publisher